Held In Contempt

An Erotic Novella

Eva Sherie

ISBN No.: 9781716017094

I am dedicating this to my husband!

#ThatIsAll

1- Kennedy (Kenni) Glory

"Objection. Leading the witness."

I really hate this muthafucka.

I tried like hell to keep my eye-roll to a minimum. Everyone I came up against already thought that I was the angry Black woman. It would be too much to just be considered a great ass lawyer. Nah. These muthafuckas always wanted to associate my success and results with the fact that everyone is afraid to piss off one of the few Black attorneys at the largest defense firm in Washington, D.C. They were all mad simply because they got their asses handed to them by a woman, a Black woman, nonetheless.

"Sustained." That time I did roll my eyes at the judge. He got on my nerves too.

I turned my attention back to the witness on the stand.

"So, you didn't see the *wet floor* cone in the aisle? Because footage shows that you not only saw the cone, you looked around, then proceeded to *slip* and yell for help. Which unfortunately led to you actually hurting yourself, but at no fault of my client, correct? You saw an opportunity and you thought you were in the clear to try and cash out." I had one goal; to show that this imbecile was committing fraud, pretending that he didn't see the wet floor cone, and proceeded to *fall* and hurt himself. Only this idiot actually tripped over his own foot in the process, really injuring himself. Meanwhile, he and his crummy ass lawyer were trying to sue my client for five million dollars. *Get the fuck outta here!*

"Objection. Badgering the witness."

Is this bitch ass dude gonna object to every damn thing I say? I mean… I may have been badgering a little, but I was irritated at the direction of this court proceeding. I also had an appointment with some good dick, so I was trying to get this shit over with.

"Sustained. Ms. Glory, please refrain from leading the witness *and* badgering the witness. I believe you are qualified enough to ask your questions in a proper manner, in ordinance with the Court of Law.

Don't you curse his ass out, Kenni. Don't do it. I stared his sexy honey-brown eyed ass right in the eye and sucked my teeth. Judge Kendrick knew he was the shit, with his fresh waves, perfectly trimmed goatee, light peanut butter skin tone, and hazel eyes. He had the looks *and* the power. He's probably just as hated as me. He's been on the bench for a while now, and these racist muthafuckas are always trying to get him out of there.

"Yes, Your Honor. My apologies." This asshole had the

nerve to sneak a wink at me. I ignored it, and the moistening in my panties, and went on with my line of questioning so I could be done with all of this. Be done with Mr. Anthony Crumm, at least until the next time we were on opposite sides, which tended to happen quite frequently. It's as if he has a damn ad somewhere that says, *Are you suing Mainline Fresh Corporation, or one of their umbrella companies? Call me now!*

At this point, I was ready to hand over this client to a colleague. That's how much I hated dealing with this dude.

Once the hearing concluded, with a win under my belt, of course, Judge Kendrick asked that I approach the bench.

"Do you need me also, Your Honor?"

Fucking ass kisser, I thought.

"Did he ask for you?"

"Ms. Glory!" Judge Kendrick boomed.

"Counselor, I don't need you at the moment. I would like to speak with Ms. Glory alone, regarding her antics in my courtroom."

"Oh well, let me get out of your hair," Anthony replied. He looked like he wanted to stick his tongue out and go *nan-nan-a-nan-nan,* like the little bitch he was.

I rolled my eyes for what seemed like the thousandth time today and followed Judge Kendrick to his chambers.

2 - Judge Andreas Kendrick

My dick was hard as a fucking rock during the entire court proceeding. Kenni played too fucking much and she knew it. I just know I am going to have to hold her in contempt one day and lock her ass up.

"Why the fuck must you keep testing me in my courtroom, Kenni?" I stared down at her sexy chocolate body. Her curves were voluptuous and enticing. I swear she tempted me with these little ass skirt suits on purpose. Kennedy's thick, luscious legs were on full display, and she wore the sexiest black pumps.

She's about to get fucked in these pumps today!

She reached to unzip my robe and made quick work of my clothes underneath.

"Because it's fun and I know you like it. I know ya dick was hard the entire time. I wish I could've climbed right up to the bench and fucked you senseless."

Before I could even get a word out, Kennedy was on her knees with my dick lodged deep in her throat.

"Damn, Kenni."

"Mmmm." She groaned around my shaft, letting her spit slide all down me. When she gripped my balls in her hand with the perfect amount of pressure, I had to lean back on my desk.

"Sss. Fuck, Kenni. Just like that. Spit on that dick."

"Yes, daddy. Feed me."

She knew how I felt when she called me *daddy*. That shit was so fucking sexy. Before she could pull the nut out of me, I gripped her ass up and laid her out on my desk, thankful that I always kept it clean and clear.

"I'm going to fuck some act right into your ass, if that's the last thing I do." I slid her skirt up, ripped her panties from her ass, and dove right into her wet pussy with my tongue.

"Yessss, daddy. Yesss."

I smacked her on her thigh while I continued to go to work. She knew that was a, *lower your fucking voice,* smack.

"I'm sorry, baby. I'm trying to be quiet."

I continued to attack her molten center, pulling her clit into my mouth and suckled, until she was creaming all on my neatly trimmed goatee. Kennedy had me so damn riled up that I knew I wasn't going to last long once I slid into her tight pussy. I also had another hearing starting in thirty minutes. Once I got her first release out the way, Kennedy would be sensitive to the slightest touch, and would be coming apart again in a matter of a few long, deep strokes.

I leaned up and gripped Kennedy's hips and slammed into her.

"Fuckkkkk, Dreeee."

I had to lean down and smother her lips with mine, making her taste herself, just to keep her from disturbing my law clerk.

"Kenni, you better shut the fuck up and take this dick. You were out there in my fucking courtroom showing the hell out. I keep telling you about that shit. You're the one that doesn't want anyone to know about us. I don't give a fuck. Keep up these games and I'm going to dead the secrecy."

"No, baby. Not yet. Ohhhhh. Shit. Shit. Shitttt." I was hitting her spot. Shit was her favorite word when she was about to come.

I pushed her leg up so far that her foot was dangling by her face.

"You gonna stop acting a fool in my courtroom?" I asked with a deep thrust. I was trying to play tough, but the way my dick was jumping deep in her walls had me thinking of the facts of my next hearing, just to maintain some control. Kennedy tried to push me away, but I smacked her hand, knocking it down. "Uh uhn. You're going to take all ten of these inches. I'm not playing with you. Don't you put your hand down there again." To prevent her from doing so, I leaned down closing the space between us, locking her extended leg in place.

"Andreas, I'm about to come. You're so deep, baby. I

can't take it."

"That's what you always say, Kenni. And every time you take this shit. Stop trying to run." And she did. Taking every stroke I threw at her, coming all over my dick, and looking sexy as hell doing so.

After Kennedy came down from her euphoric haze, she squeezed her pussy muscles and I was done. Her pussy sucked me in and gripped me like a pair of warm, gushy pliers, wringing me out.

"Kenni. Shit, girl. I'm about to..."

"That's right daddy. Don't forget about the power of this pussy. Come for me." She must've been over my shit talking and wanted to put her own powers on display, because I couldn't hold back the grunt and letting my seed flow deep into her womb.

"Damn! You better be lucky Renee knows about us and can keep her mouth shut. If you're going to continue to act up in my courtroom and need to be fucked after, you're going to have to keep those screams down."

"You're gonna have to keep those strokes shallow."

"Never." I kissed Kennedy on the lips and helped her get cleaned up and walked her to the door.

"No more antics, Ms. Glory," I said to her loud enough for everyone outside my chambers to hear me *scold* her.

"Yes, Your Honor. Again, my apologies."

Kennedy strolled her big, juicy ass out my office trying to control her, *I just got fucked,* walk. I let out a chuckle and focused back on my schedule for the rest of the day. I'm sure I would be seeing Ms. Glory soon.

3 - *Kennedy*

I pulled up to my office and parked my G- Wagen in my designated spot… the benefits of making partner. I needed to see what else required my attention the day, before I made it to my evening dick appointment. I would have all the time in the world for that one; no quickies.

Jameela, my legal assistant was ready and waiting for me. Probably with some shit that would mess up the rest of my afternoon. But I wouldn't get too irritated with her. Her and I became really close over the past three years. She had my back in everything, and dealt with all of my professional and personal matters.

"Hey Meela. Anything crazy happened while I was in court?"

"If you call Anthony Crumm sending over an email, cc'ing all of the partners, informing them of your unprofessionalism, and how you were reprimanded by Judge Kendrick, crazy… then yup."

"I really hate that guy! Like, why does he live to make my life miserable. I just don't understand."

"Oh, and he also stated that he was going to be appealing the ruling. Stating that you bullied his client to make false statements and in turn persuaded the jury."

"Urghhhhh. Why is this my life?"

I threw myself back into my seat, beyond pissed at the thought of having to do the same trial all over again.

"You had to have done something to him, Kenni. He would not be targeting you this hard for nothing."

"Meela, I've thought the same thing. But I swear, I didn't know his ass before arguing on opposite sides in court."

Jameela shrugged. "I just don't believe his vendetta just came out of nowhere. I'll see if I can gather some background info on him… try to put together these missing puzzle pieces."

"Knock yourself out. I don't really give a fuck about Anthony Crumm. All I know is, if he keeps fucking with me, he's going to meet the Kenni from the block, and my cousins!"

"You would not have that man jumped, Kennedy!"

"Shitttt. Don't let those degrees hangin' on the wall fool you. I'm straight Southeast D.C. bred… that nigga keep testing my gangsta and I have quite a few people I could hit up."

Jameela laughed so hard. "Whatever, Kenni."

She thought I was playing, but I was deadass serious.

"Well, I'll let you get to it. I know you have your *appointment* at the Four Seasons later."

"Yes, girl! The spa is calling me." I winked at Meela.

"Yeah, okay. Tell Mr. Spa I said hello."

"Will do."

For the rest of the afternoon I caught up on emails and finalized a few pleadings. I was so excited to hit I95 North for the fifty-minute trip to Baltimore. For as long as I could remember, this was my second Friday outing every moth.

Packing up my things, I left my office earlier than any other day. I was normally here until seven or eight at night, but not on the second Friday of each month. My ass was out of here at four o'clock, at the latest, for my monthly *appointment*.

"Meela, I'm getting ready to head out. You can leave early if there's nothing pressing you need to get out. Enjoy your weekend and I'll see you on Monday."

"Byeee, Kenni… have fun," Jameela sang.

I flipped her the bird and walked out.

~~~~~

I walked into the lobby of the Four Seasons feeling like a million bucks. I lifted my Dior shades, set them on top of my curly, shoulder length locs, and proceeded to strut up to the check-in desk with my Louboutin's clacking against the marble flooring.

"Good evening Ms. Glory. I already have you checked in. Here's your room key."

Tina was always on shift when I checked in for my little rendezvous and was so nice. I could see the curiosity behind her
~~~~~

lids, but her professionalism would never allow her to inquire.

"Thanks, Tina. Have a great evening."

"You also, ma'am."

Even though she was old enough to probably be my mother, Tina always addressed me as ma'am no matter how many times I tried to correct her. So, I just stopped.

When I stepped into the luxury suite, there was an assortment of fragrant flowers strategically placed all over, releasing a calming aroma. There was a note on the coffee table.

Agápi Mou (My Love)- I'm running a little late, beautiful. I have a spa treatment for you starting at six-thirty. I'll be there by the time your pampering is done.

He always knew how to make a girl feel special. These Friday nights were everything. It was so nice to come down from tireless litigation, to this euphoric atmosphere. I made sure to get myself pampering fresh and to be ready before the spa staff arrived.

~~~~~

The masseuse was amazing, and I was completely relaxed. I was on my way into a deep sleep when I felt the pressure change. The person's touch felt stronger, more masculine. I knew immediately that my bae had arrived. Unlike the masseuse, he went straight for my ass, rubbing and spreading my cheeks apart.
~~~~~

“Hey, baby,” he whispered in my ear.

“Mmm… hi, babe. Don’t stop. That feels so good.”

“Yea? How about this?” He asked, as he slipped his middle finger into my throbbing center and I ached for more of his touch.

I know I just had sex earlier in the day, but this right here was what I really needed. Hours of my body being the center of attention.

“Turn over and spread them legs, baby.”

I shuffled my ass right into place, and I watched as he squirted edible oil all down the front of my body. My babe massaged my neck and applied pressure as he kissed me sensually. Our tongues tangled with one another, expertly exploring. The kiss was so damn sexy, that it had me coming.

“Shit, baby.”

“That’s it Agápi (love). I’m going to put that ass to the test tonight.”

All I could do was moan. So far, I had only been kissed and penetrated with a middle finger, and I was already on cloud nine. Our appointment was always this explosive, but it still felt like the first time, every time. When he tweaked one nipple and sucked hard on the other one, my back bowed off of the massage table as if I were possessed.

“Baby, I need you to fuck me.”

"Shh. Not yet. I want to finish your massage."

My body was touched, rubbed, licked, and teased until every inch of me felt the burn my baby's hands left behind. My entire body was ignited, and the heat danced across my sensitive skin, causing beads of perspiration to cover my body.

When my babe was done with his sensual assault on the massage table, he picked me up and carried me to the bed, and I melted into the plush mattress. Next thing I knew, I was being blindfolded. There were a few quiet moments before I heard music playing throughout the suite. Avant's *Make Good Love* kicked off what I knew was about to be an epic night.

I felt the bed dip, then heard a buzz. I wanted to snatch the mask off my damn face to see what the hell was buzzing. But I refrained, and I didn't have to wait too long to figure out what it was, because I felt what I believed to be a bullet making contact with my clit. That shit had me ready to jump off the bed.

"Don't make me handcuff your ass to this bed, Kennedy."

I knew his ass would make good on his threat and cuff me, so I relaxed my body, and breathed through my impending orgasm.

"That's it, baby. Spread your legs wider."

I happily obliged, because I knew he was about to eat me up in the best possible way.

"I want that nectar on my tongue; can't let it go to waste."

That first long lick had me wanting to bow off of the bed again, however, I controlled it because I didn't want to be cuffed or tied down. Not that I didn't like being bound, because every now and again I was with it as long as I knew it was coming… I had a thing with control. However, in the current moment, I wanted to be able to roam my hands freely over his body while he delivered mind blowing orgasms.

"Mmm. You taste so sweet."

Because I eat my pineapples and mangos and drink water, I thought. It was a fleeting thought though, because when he pulled my clit into his mouth and stuck the vibrator deep inside my center, I creamed all over his face.

"God. Baby, I can't take it. I can't take it."

"Yes, you can, and you will."

I thought he would let up once my release subsided, but he didn't. My baby went right back to work, focusing his tongue on my entrance and moving it in slow wide circles in and out of my swollen core. Although I was blindfolded, I squeezed my eyes shut, trying to breathe through my third orgasm.

"That's it. Fill me up, Kennedy."

I filled his ass up on all that I had to offer. I came so hard in his mouth, holding his head in place to make sure every drop was caught.

I felt him leave the bed, and my mind raced, trying to

anticipate what he would do next. Then there he was, straddling my upper body, rubbing the thick mushroomed head of his dick at my mouth. I opened wide and was fed a copious amount of his thickness. I suctioned my mouth and pulled him in even deeper. A simple blindfold wasn't going to stop me from trying to gain some control.

"Fuck, Kennedy," he spewed, as he fucked my face faster.

I took it all, wanting to please my baby as much as he pleased me. I knew I had him when I reached up and grabbed his ass and pulled him into my mouth as deep as he could go. I felt him touching my tonsils, and it took major concentration to control my gag reflexes. Babe pulled out, snatched my blindfold off, and stroked his release onto my lips and down my throat, with some landing on my chin. It was so much nut that it oozed out the side of my mouth before I could catch it all.

I thought I would have a moment to rest, after that release. Nope. My baby was still hard when he finished spurting down my throat.

Before I knew it, I was being flipped over and he drove into me hard from behind. I just knew the entire damn floor of the Four Seasons heard my screams of pleasure. He was relentless in his pursuit to pull even more pleasure from me.

Smacking me hard on the ass, he gritted out, "Hands."

I got excited and was ready to come just from that

command. This was one of his signature moves and I loved it. I threw my arms behind me, and he gripped each of my wrists in his large hands. I, in turn, wrapped my hands around his wrists and held on for the ride I knew would commence.

Holding tight with my arms locked behind me, he thrust so deep into me. I swear I could feel his dick in my stomach. He loved gripping me up like this because I couldn't thwart his strokes in this position. I currently didn't want to, because with each stroke, my G-spot was getting all the attention she loved and deserved.

"Babyyyyy. Shitttt. I'm cominggggg!" I screamed. He continued to fuck me through orgasm number four, and I swear I blacked out for a few seconds after that one. When I came down, he let my arms go and leaned his body down over mine, gripping my neck in his large palm, and turning my head to the side.

"I fucking love this pussy. I fucking love you."

After that, all I could make out was inaudible grunts as he came deep inside my walls.

We went on like this until the sun started to creep on the horizon. I knew I was going to need to sleep most of the Saturday, just like after every other rendezvous.

4 - Andreas

I woke up with her beautiful cocoa body splayed across my chest. I took a moment and thought about how it always feels so good when we get these secret visits in. It was the allure of booking a hotel suite for the weekend and fucking like crazy, that had my dick standing at attention at the moment. However, I needed to get my morning workout in. I never missed them, even after draining all of my energy for hours. So instead of waking Kennedy up with my dick embedded in her tight pussy or warm mouth, I took a breath and attempted to get ahold of myself.

"Kenni. Wake up."

"Noooo. Can't you skip your workout for once? Stay in bed with me."

"I'll be right back here by your side before you wake, baby. But you know the deal."

She groaned and rolled her body off mine, allowing me to escape the bed. Surprisingly, Kennedy opened her eyes and stared at me. She was normally knocked out, and most times didn't even feel me climb out of bed for my workout.

Since I had her full attention, me and my dick, I broached a topic we fought about often.

"Don't you think it's time we stop sneaking off to Baltimore for these monthly dates? Or at least let our colleagues know we're together so we don't have to drive an hour away for some peaceful time alone outside of the house."

"Not yet Dre. I'm not ready. I want to make it to the top before anyone knows I'm associated with you. I want my hard work to be noticed. I don't want people to think, *oh another Black girl fucking her way to the top.*"

"Fuck them! You work hard, if not harder, than everyone at your damn firm. You graduated top of your class from Stanford University. You made it out of Southeast D.C. all on your own, before you even laid eyes on me."

"We know all of this, but the masses won't know that. And quite frankly, I don't think they will give a damn."

Frustrated with the conversation, per usual, I went and took a quick shower before heading to the gym. I needed to at least wash the dried come from my body, brush my teeth and take care of Kennedy's sweet cream moisturizing my goatee. I knew I was going to the gym to sweat, but I didn't want to be in there smelling like badussy, on top of workout funk.

"Whatever, Kennedy. Same shit different day. Let's forget we even had this conversation and go on with enjoying the rest of the weekend." This fucking suite cost me a thousand dollars just for two nights, I wasn't about to spend that shit arguing with her stubborn ass. “I want your ass showered and naked when I get back. Oh, and call housekeeping to change them sheets. I’m gonna need fresh ones to fuck you on.”

Before she could respond I closed the door to the massive en suite bathroom.

~~~~~

I returned to the room about two hours later, after an intense lifting session. When I opened the door to the bedroom, everything was neat and clean, but I didn’t see Kennedy anywhere. I know her ass ain’t get mad and leave, so I headed for the shower.

When I opened the bathroom door there were dozens of little candles all over, and the bathtub was filled with water. Kennedy sat on the edge of the tub in her birthday suit with a mimosa in her hand.

“You’re right on time, daddy,” she said and winked at me.

I climbed my ass up out of my sweaty gym clothes, walked over to her with my hard dick swinging back and forth, and leaned down and kissed her on the forehead.

“I fucking love your ass girl.”

“I know. I love you, too. And I don’t ever want you to think that I don’t love you because of the situation I’m putting us in.”

“Know that I’ll never doubt your love. I know shit has
~~~~~

been fucked up for you and you get treated like shit out here as a successful Black woman. I get you wanting to establish your legacy before outwardly intertwining it with mine. If anything, I respect you more for wanting to establish your brand on your own and not want to attach yourself to me to better yourself. I fell in love with your independence. And even though you don't need me to further your career or need my money. I know you still need me in the stands cheering you on. Know that I will always have your back whether muthafuckas know it or not."

"I love you so much, baby."

"We already established that. I'm assuming this bath water is for us to enjoy… let's get in before it gets cold. I know you made that shit skin melting hot."

Kennedy laughed her beautiful laugh and said, "Shut up, Andreas."

It wasn't too long after we climbed in that Kennedy was riding my dick. Whenever we were around each other naked, we were fucking in less than five minutes.

"Damn, you know how to ride this dick, Kenni." I leaned my head back on the headrest and enjoyed Kennedy's strong ass knees and tight ass pussy.

"You gonna come for me, daddy?"

I grunted. "Not until you come first." That was going to be a feat because I was ready to release right that moment.

“Nah. That’s not how this is going to work this time around. You have all weekend to make me weak with this big dick of yours. Right now, though, you're gonna give me this nut.”

Kennedy squeezed her pussy muscles and I had no choice but to oblige.

“Got-damn, Kenni!” I leaned into her and bit into the crook of her shoulder to keep from further crying out like a little bitch. It never ceased to amaze me at how Kennedy could have me coming undone.

5 - Kennedy

I walked into my office feeling like a new woman who had been expertly fucked for forty-eight hours straight, with snack breaks. I was ready to attack anything that came at me. No depressed ass, *Urgh, it's Monday,* chants for me.

"Good moringggg, Jameela," I sang.

She laughed at me. "I take it your weekend appointment went well."

"It went wonderfully. You have a good weekend?"

"I did. I'm sure not as fun as yours, but I can't complain. I actually had a little bit of free time and we need to chat about your boy Anthony Crumm."

"It's too early!" I whined and walked to my office. Jameela closed the door behind her and plopped down on the loveseat.

"Trust me… you wanna hear this."

I sat down and waved my hand in the air, letting her know to proceed. She was giddy as hell about whatever it was she found out.

"Girl!" She started excitedly. I had to laugh at her antics. Jameela was my girl and because we had similar backgrounds we stuck together in the office, making the workday fun.

"So, this loser went to Stanford with you; even graduated the same year. I stalked all of his social media pages and found some juicy stuff."

"Really? I feel like I would remember him. Also, I guess I never really cared about him as an attorney to know where he went to school. I normally look up that info, but whatever. What else you got? That can't have anything to do with the reason for him hating me."

"No, listen... homeboy has really been on some white privilege shit his entire life. I found old tweets about how much he hates Affirmative Action, and even deeper, he really hates Black women. One tweet from his second year of law school read, *It's not enough that I have to unjustly compete with these fatherless niggers, I also have to compete with these nigger bitches too*. I don't even know how no one found that tweet yet and blasted his ass. I guess no one has as many lonely nights and free time on their hands as much as me. Anyways, I digress. I bet if you pull up your old law school ranking, he's behind your ass. I'll even bet he's close behind you, which really ignites his hatred for you... apart from you being Black, of course."

"Damn. That's some heavy shit." I was stunned. By both Anthony Crumm's racist background and Jameela's detective work. Who has that much damn time on their hands?

I'm really gonna have to get her some dick, and soon!

"Right!" She continued, completely oblivious to my thoughts. "What do you want to do with this information?"

"Nothing yet. Let's just hold on to it for now. So far, he's only been a little thorn in my side. I have a feeling it'll get worse if he keeps losing to me. I like the idea of having this in my back pocket for when he really steps out of line."

"Sounds good. I'll see if I can dig up some more info."

"Girl, I really need to get you some dick." I couldn't hold onto my earlier thoughts any longer. My friend needed help.

"We can't all get knocked down by a sexy ass judge," Jameela whispered like the door wasn't closed.

I threw a pen at her ass.

"Shut the fuck up!"

There were only a handful of people who knew of my involvement with Andreas, and Jameela was one of them. I trusted her with everything in me.

"Abuse. I'm going back to my damn desk!"

6 - Andreas

I was relaxing in Shelly's Back Room, enjoying a cigar, and winding down from a long day of court hearings. I wasn't a man who had many friends; thus, I enjoyed the peaceful moments to myself.

Thoughts of Kennedy were running rampant through my mind. Her beautiful, silky chocolate skin, her neatly twisted locs, her sexy round face, and full pouty lips... everything about her just called to me. I didn't know how much longer I would be able to live with our relationship being a secret. I wanted to claim her as mine in and outside of the bedroom.

Just as my thoughts were veering into what we do in the bedroom, and I use that term loosely because we fuck everywhere, I was interrupted.

"Judge Kendrick. Fancy running into you here."

I puffed on my cigar and blew the smoke out slowly, finally giving my attention to a man that I could not stand.

"Mr. Crumm. Good evening."

"Please, call me Anthony. We're not in your courtroom."

I nodded, and could tell that he was waiting for me to extend the same luxury. I would never.

"What can I do for you, Anthony?"

He looked taken aback by my question. His cheeks

started to turn pink with what I assumed was embarrassment.

"Nothing at all, sir. I just saw you sitting over here and thought I'd join you."

He sounded like he was spitting some dumb ass line at a female, and I was ready to send him on his way. However, something in me gave pause and I was curious to see what he wanted. Gesturing to the empty seat beside me, "Have a seat, Anthony."

"Oh, thank you, sir."

I was glad that he didn't feel comfortable enough to attempt to call me by my first name, because I would have put an immediate stop to that shit. In no way did I want him to think we were friends. The only reason he was sitting here was because it looked like he had something to get off his chest.

After the initial small talk, and a glass of whiskey, I guess Anthony got comfortable enough to speak freely.

"So how did your reprimand of Kennedy Glory go last week?"

That had my senses on full alert. I could feel the bullshit coming.

"That was a private in chamber discussion, that I will not discuss outside of those four walls."

If Anthony had been paying closer attention, he would have caught on to my demeanor and moved to another subject.

Of course, he did not.

"Well, I hope she takes heed to whatever you said, because she can be a real bitch."

I wanted to lay his ass out as soon as those words left his mouth. But I would not put my career on the line. Every White judge in D.C. Superior Court was already looking for a way to get my ass out of there.

"Mr. Crumm in no uncertain terms will you speak on any women in my presence in that manner. You most certainly will not speak on your fellow attorney, who you do business with on a regular basis, that way. I absolutely do not tolerate any disrespect of women, especially Black women."

I raised up out the chair, buttoned my suit jacket, and headed for the door. I could have sworn I heard him mumble, *fucking nigger,* but I knew I was trippin' because ole boy wasn't that damn stupid.

~~~~~

When I pulled into the driveway, I noticed Kennedy's truck already parked. That made me feel good.

"Mmm. I'm glad to see you here," I told her when she reached out to grab my briefcase from my hands.

"Whatever, Dre," she laughed. "I made your favorite. I have the table all set."

"I could always eat," I told her suggestively and pulled
~~~~~

her into me for a kiss.

"Mmm. Stop playing and let's eat."

"Who said I wasn't about to eat?" I picked her up and carried her to the kitchen as she squealed.

"Andreas Kendrick, you better put me down!"

"Or what?"

"Or you won't get dessert."

"Baby, all of this chocolatiness is dessert." With that, I sat her on the island and spread her legs wide. My dick just about jumped out of my slacks when I saw she didn't have any panties on and had a freshly waxed pussy.

"You must have wanted me to feast on this shit. Got this sexy ass strip directing me right to where you want me to be." Her pussy lips were dripping with her arousal and the sweet aroma filled my nostrils. I couldn't wait for a taste.

"Andreas, the food is getting cold."

"That's what the fuck microwaves and ovens are for." Any other protests died on her lips as I sucked her swollen pearl into my mouth and fed myself dessert before the main course… I planned to have that too, but I needed to relieve the day's stress and making my woman come did that shit for me.

7 - Kennedy

After *dessert,* we settled at the dining room table for Andreas' favorite, seared rack of lamb, homemade mashed potatoes, and roasted asparagus. He didn't really care what sides were served, but lamb was his favorite meat to indulge in. Especially since he only allowed himself to eat meat once a week. Other days he ate plant based and I wasn't with that shit. I wanted all the cows, lambs, chickens… whatever.

"How was your day today? Thankfully I got a break from the courthouse, which I needed, but I could've used a little sneak session in your chambers."

"Kenni you are so damn insatiable. We just spent an entire weekend fucking."

I looked at him as if he were crazy.

"So…"

Andreas laughed at me and shook his head.

"Anyway, girl. You're never going to guess who I ran into while winding down at the cigar lounge."

"Who?" I asked.

"Anthony Crumm."

Kennedy thought for a moment if she should share the information she knew. She decided to hold on to it a little longer, and keep it to herself.

"That's interesting. What did he want?"

"To talk about you and how I reprimanded you."

"And did you tell him how you waxed this ass all over your desk?"

Andreas raised his brow and took a sip of the whiskey I had poured for him.

"I didn't know that I could. Because with the shit he was talking, I was milliseconds from telling him he was disrespecting my fucking woman."

"I was just joking, Andreas."

I don't even know why I said that shit. I know he's about to start the age-old argument.

"But I'm not. You know how I feel about this shit, Kennedy."

"I know. I know. I'm not ready yet."

I could see the disappointment in his eyes. He really wanted the world to know about us, but I still had a road to pave, on my own, before the entire city diminished my hard work and success behind a man I was involved with.

"I don't want to fight. Let's just finish our dinner."

I exhaled a huge breath, knowing I was hurting him by keeping our situation a secret.

"Baby, you know I love you, right?"

"I have never or will ever question that shit, Kenni. I know you love me, and I know you want to be with me. I also understand where you are coming from. However, I do think we should get ahead of this before someone else finds out."

"Someone would have to be lurking really damn hard. I know that's not the point, and I hear where you're coming from. Let me think about it, okay."

"I've been a patient man this long, baby. I can wait a little longer."

"Thank you, love. Are you finished?" It was a rhetorical question because his plate was completely bare. I got up and cleared the table and did a quick wipe down of the kitchen. Andreas hated when I left the kitchen a mess.

My little neat freak judge, I thought to myself.

Now that we had dinner out the way, and our normal disagreement, I could go on and finish feeding him his dessert. It was so crazy how I could never get enough of him. If I could let that man spread me open every day, multiple times a day, I would. However, every now and again my coochie will tell a bitch to chill, soak, and give her a break. I would begrudgingly listen.

"Come on, let's head upstairs."

Andreas followed my lead, already knowing where my mind was. He loved fucking me just as much as I loved being fucked by him.

When he opened the door, there was shock on his face.

"You so graciously gave me a nice massage on Friday, and I thought I would return the favor. Go get showered and I'll be right here waiting for you."

Andreas walked into the adjoining bathroom and seconds later I heard the showerhead running. I wanted to get in there with him, even though I showered before he got home. Shower sex with Andreas was always one of my favorites. The way his big strong arms would lift me, and he'd stroke me into oblivion, while the hot water pounded down on us, always turned me on.

I knew his ass was excited about what was about to transpire, because his shower was much shorter than normal. He walked out of the bathroom with a towel wrapped around his waist and droplets of water peppering his chest. He looked so good, and I wanted to lick up each little droplet. I controlled my hormones so I could give my man a much-deserved massage.

I wouldn't be myself if I didn't fuck with him though.

"Did you make sure you got all the hotspots? That shower was short as hell."

"Ha. Ha," he retorted dryly. "You always got jokes."

Laughing, I waved for him to get up on the table face down. I wanted to start with his back, because when I got to his front, I was going to massage and lick him everywhere, like my thoughts from moments ago.

I stopped by my favorite sex shop and stocked up on all

kinds of goodies for tonight, including edible body oils. A sista was going to be tired as hell at work tomorrow. But spending time with my man was always worth it.

As I started my massage at his neck and shoulders, I noticed how tight he was. I felt somewhat guilty because I knew I contributed to his stress. However, I was going to focus on massaging and fucking it out of him tonight.

"Damn, Kenni, that feels good as hell."

"I'm known to give a good massage or two."

"Yeah, well I better be the only muthafucka getting those massages now. I don't want to have to step down from my bench and fuck a nigga up."

"Ohhh, look at the Philly hood dude making a rare appearance. I love it!"

"As long as you know, Kenni."

"Baby, I would never test your gangsta. I am not fooled by that robe and gavel."

Once I finished massaging his back, I instructed him to turn over. I climbed on top of him and straddled his waist as I massaged his upper body. Andreas kept trying to grab a hold of my hips, but I continuously smacked his hands away.

"Just enjoy, baby."

I know he could feel the heat emanating from my pussy. I was turned on and wet as fuck, but I played it off and stayed the ever-focused masseuse. When I turned around and straddled him in reverse cowboy style to massage his lower half, Andreas let out a long groan. The view displayed before him was making his dick grow even harder under me. As I leaned forward to massage his calves and feet, he couldn't help but to rub on my round, plump ass. I massaged and gyrated on him until he couldn't take it anymore. Andreas lifted my ass up and slid into me with one long thrust of his hips. He spread my ass cheeks and guiding me up and down his long thick dick.

"Fuckkkk, Andreas. I wasn't finished with my massage."

"Fuck that massage. The way you were bouncing this ass on my dick, you wanted me to slide up in here."

He was absolutely right. I wanted to drive him wild. We worked the shit out of that massage table switching from position to position. I knew I wanted to make the night about him, but his ass showed me. Andreas had me coming back to back to back. He finally released his load on my stomach as I laid on my back on the table, with him between my legs. The look of pure bliss on his face made my pussy cream even more. Making him feel good, made me feel good.

"Damn, Dre. I was supposed to suck all of that up outta you. You hijacked my plans."

"There's always tomorrow. Let's go get in the shower. That shit just drained all my energy and a brotha needs to go the hell to bed."

I laughed at him. But I was also drained and ready for sleep. So that's what we did. After getting lost in one another, we cleansed our bodies, eased our minds, and fell asleep in one another's arms.

8 - Kennedy

Another case won!

I was inwardly jumping for joy, patting myself on the back, giving myself a pound… yeah... all of that. I was on a hot streak. Every case I argued before the court in the last six months, I have won. There were some cases I settled before we got to trial because I knew my ass would lose, and I wasn't about that life. So, I don't consider that losing. Both sides win. Injured parties get some money, my clients spend way less than what they would on court fees, and aren't hit with multi-million-dollar judgments, on top of paying me top dollar. Everyone wins in that scenario. I only take that route when I know there's more than a thirty percent chance I'll lose.

I settled back in my chair, basking in another victory, and thought about the past few weeks. Life had been great. Andreas and I were in a great place, not that we've ever been in a bad place, but lately he's even laid off talks of going public with our relationship. That shit made my pussy twitch. I mean, he always had my pussy twitching and creaming, but that right there kept if flowing like the Nile, knowing our secrecy was bothering him less.

When I got a moment, I needed to send a quick shout out to God and my IUD for keeping me from being barefoot, pregnant, and in the kitchen. Not that I didn't want kids, one day, I just didn't want them anytime soon. But one day, I would let Andreas knock me up with one of his little half Greek babies.

Thinking of having babies, made me think of Andreas' parents. I was always amused when I looked at their pictures, images of the world's most mixed-matched couple. His dad was this tall bulky dark chocolate man, and his mother was a tiny Greek woman, probably not even topping five feet tall. But I had to thank them both for creating the Adonis that is Andreas, because that man wasn't just a beautiful specimen, he was cultured, intelligent, and had that big dick swag.

I had to catch myself, because my mind was really running away with me and I needed to get it together for my next scheduled trial, which happened to be up against no other than crummy ass Anthony Crumm. I really did not feel like dealing with that man. It seemed like he's made it his life's mission to be a thorn in my got-damn side. I still had a hard time believing that his ill feelings toward me stemmed from some college shit. I found that to be super immature and some extra White privilege madness.

"Good afternoon Ms. Glory," Jameela sang. She was away from her desk when I got back into the office, but by her sing-song tone, I figured she got the news about my trial.

"Ms. Sparrow, how are you on this glorious afternoon?"

We both burst out laughing over our own antics. It was like being a comedian and laughing at your own jokes… just sad. But that was our relationship, and I wouldn't change it for anything.

"Girl, I heard you kicked butt today! You're back early. No post hearing rendezvous?"

"Not today, even though I could've used a little celebratory lovin'. However, Andreas didn't preside over this trial, the courthouse was busy, and it would have looked really suspect of me to waltz into his chambers and shut the door behind me."

"I can see that looking really inappropriate. Anyways, are you ready for Anthony Crumm and his lying ass client?"

"Yup, sure am. Were you able to get the footage from the traffic light?"

"Got it today, and it shows his client cutting off the Mainline truck, causing the collision." Meela said and did a little happy dance.

"BINGO!" That video was exactly what I needed to shove this case down Anthony's throat. I can be queen of petty when provoked, okay I'm lying, I can just be queen of petty for no damn reason. And I wanted to sit high on that throne right now.

"I wish we didn't have to supplement this shit to him and

the judge, and pop up with it on some surprise stuff like in the movies. I would love that."

Jameela laughed and shook her head.

"You are truly a mess. Can I please come to the hearing?"

Jameela loved to join me in court when she knew a case was going to be particularly juicy. And I always let her. She'd sit behind me and have each of my exhibits ready before I even asked. Honestly, I should probably take her behind to court with me every time.

"Sure. I'll let the partners know."

"Yes!"

"Girl, calm your ass down and let's get this case airtight for the jurors. Do we know who this case is being heard in front of?"

"Yup," Jameela smirked. Her look told me all that I needed. My boo was presiding over this case.

Oh, I'ma have some fun with this one.

We settled into my office with papers spread out everywhere, marking potential exhibits, and getting ready to come out victoriously over Anthony Crumm, again.

9 - Andreas

When I saw Kennedy had another trial scheduled with Crumm's shady ass, I made sure my law clerk knew to do whatever he needed to get the case on my docket. I had to do that for two reasons: 1. Kennedy was liable to be held in contempt in another judge's courtroom for the aggressive tactics she likes to use when going up against Anthony; 2. I wanted to watch his ass after his racist comments that night in the cigar lounge. I'd love to throw his ass in jail for any disrespectful outbursts he may have.

As everyone was filling into the courtroom, I said a quick little prayer, asking God to not make me have to throw Kennedy's ass in jail, right along with Crumm. Pre-motions were argued, the jury instructions were read to the jurors, and the case kicked off with openings. I previously reviewed the exhibits, probably a little more thoroughly than I would have for any other case, but I knew Kennedy would have this case in the bag, just from the video she recently produced.

When it was time for Anthony's client to take the stand, I saw the evil gleam in Kennedy's eyes and threw up another prayer.

"In your deposition Mr. Smith, you testified that Mr. Peters hit you from behind, correct?"

"Objection."

"On what grounds?" Kennedy turned and gave Anthony a death glare.

"You're answering the question for him."

I gripped the bridge of my nose because these two fools were acting like children arguing over every damn thing. I know Kennedy had been provoked for a long time by Anthony, but I just wished she'd chill a little bit. The objection was bullshit, but in an attempt to not show favoritism, I agreed with this snake dude.

"Sustained," I breathed out. "Ms. Glory, please rephrase your question."

Kennedy let out her own breath, but composed herself quickly. This damn hearing was going to stop me from getting some pussy tonight… I could already see it.

"I can do even better, Your Honor. I would like to enter Exhibit 13; will the jury please focus their attention on the projector."

Jameela was ready, with the laptop set up and hit play.

"So, Mr. Smith, my question to you is… Is that you in your vehicle waiting to pull out into traffic?"

The witness started to move around in his seat uncomfortably, and hesitated to answer the question.

"Your Honor," Kennedy spoke to me and waved her hand

at the witness.

"Mr. Smith, please answer Ms. Glory's question."

"Yes, that is me."

Anthony Crumm was sitting behind the plaintiff's desk turning beet red.

"Okay, and if we watch for about another twenty seconds," She paused, allowing the footage to continue, "There… Is that you pulling out into oncoming traffic, in front of Mr. Peters truck?"

"Objection."

This time I had to ask what for because there wasn't one reason why this line of questioning deserved an objection. Anthony just stuttered trying to throw whatever would stick, I'm sure to try and distract the jury.

"Overruled. Mr. Smith, please answer the question."

"He… he… he wasn't that close when I pulled out. Mr. Peters sped up on purpose."

"So, you are saying that my client purposely accelerated to cause the collision?"

"Yes. That's what I am saying."

"Okay, Mr. Smith… I am not sure if you are aware, but I will inform you that if a collision was premeditated, the insurance company is not liable for the actions of the insured, your counsel would have filed his lawsuit in the wrong department. But that's neither here nor there, I simply need a yes or no answer. Is that you, pulling out into oncoming traffic, in front of Mr. Peters truck?"

"Yes."

"No further questions, Your Honor."

Kennedy strutted her sexy ass back to her seat and smiled at Anthony the entire time.

During closing arguments, Kennedy mentioned that her client was not responsible, regardless of whichever story they believed of the Plaintiff, due to him driving into oncoming traffic, and if he in fact believed it was intentional, she pointed the jury to the clause in the insurance policy that clearly stated all intentional acts were not covered by the company. While Anthony chose to focus on Kennedy and her aggressive and bullying nature. I guess he figured he'd make Kennedy look bad to the jury so they wouldn't be compelled to rule in her favor. However, it just made Anthony look like he was weak, unprofessional, and a sore loser. With all of that, it was no surprise the jury came back with a verdict in favor of Kennedy and her client.

I just wanted all of these muthafuckas out of my courtroom. I was tired of all the bickering. I wanted to call Kennedy back into my chambers, but I noticed Anthony Crumm staring at her with laser focus. I knew any communication with her would be observed very closely.

Kennedy smiled, and licked her lips at me before walking out of the courtroom. I gave a little half smile back, knowing I was going to tear her ass up later tonight.

10 - Kennedy

"You're sexy as hell when you're handing muthafuckas their asses in the courtroom. I be wanting to bend your ass over my bench and fuck the shit out of you. And you better stop wearing those tiny ass skirt suits in my courtroom. I know you do that shit on purpose. I've seen you in the courthouse before other judges, you don't wear that shit then."

Andreas had my ass gripped up against the huge island in the kitchen. His hands were on the back of my neck and he had me bent over. I guess because he couldn't bend me over his bench, he'd settle for his kitchen island. He hovered over my body and was continuously talking dirty to me. I heard him rustling with something and then the sound of something clinking against the counter got my attention. I tried to turn my head and see what type of freaky shit Andreas was about to be on, but he applied more pressure to his grip, preventing me from satisfying my curiosity.

Next thing I knew, this fucking man was pulling my hands above my head and handcuffing them to the sink. Andreas knew I had a thing about control. Not that I minded giving it to him, but I would have at least liked to have been prepared.

"Andreas, what the fuck are you doing?"

I pulled against the cuffs to test how restricted I actually was, and realized my ass wasn't going any damn where. The island was too wide for me to try and maneuver the cuff over the curve of the faucet. I was stretched out with my bare chest flat against the quartz countertop.

"Damn, Kenni, you look good enough to eat splayed out like this. You know, I think I will have a snack."

Andreas gently kicked my legs farther apart, leaving me open and exposed to him.

"Nigga, what are you, a cop now? Are you about to search me?" I said through a chuckle. That chuckle died right on my lips as soon as I felt his tongue snake it's way between my folds. "Shitttt. Dre. I wasn't ready."

"Get ready Kenni, because I'm gonna taste this pussy, my pussy, all fucking night long."

And I swear my ass was bent over in this position for what felt like an eternity while he sucked every last drop of nectar from my sweet center. My legs felt like jelly and I was ready to tap completely out, but Dre wouldn't let me. I pleaded with him to give me a break. The only intermission he provided was giving my swollen bud a break, but still focusing on the rest of my slippery folds. My voice was hoarse from crying out in pleasure for so long.

"Baby, please…" I cried out for what seemed like the

hundredth time. Andreas suddenly stopped his assault and I could finally take a breather. That didn't last long, though, because he slid his dick deep inside my walls. The depths he reached with his amazing shaft had me seeing stars. I don't know if I was imagining it, or if I could really feel him deep in my stomach.

"Ahhhhh," I squeaked when he pulled back and slid back in. The feel of him didn't just fill my honeypot, Andreas' essence surrounded each and every inch of my entire being. He heated me from the inside out, causing a layer of sheen to cover my body and prickle all of my senses.

"This is what I want to do to you after every time you leave my courtroom, Kenni. All I can think about is burying my dick deep in your tight ass walls."

"Babyyyyyy," My throat was so raw that I could barely croak out the word.

Andreas continued to stroke me at an even pace, but continued to go as deep as he could. Not before long, we were both on the precipice of an amazing release, jumping into the abyss of endless pleasure.

Once our euphoric haze eased, Andreas uncuffed me and massaged my wrists. They were sore, but I wouldn't change a damn thing. He carried me upstairs, and we took a bath together, continuing to cloak ourselves in endless ecstasy for hours.

~~~~~
~~~~~

I woke up the next morning and stretched my limbs. It felt like I had been hit by a Mack truck, but I wouldn't have it any other way. Andreas was gone for his early morning workout. One of these days I was going to get him to lay in bed with me. He'd eventually make it back to bed and cuddle with me, but not before he got in at least an hour or two at the gym.

I decided to lay back and watch the news before getting up and getting ready for work. As soon as I turned the T.V. to the local news channel, I let the remote slip from my hand and bought it to cover my mouth in complete and utter shock.

Breaking News! You're hearing it here first on, WUSA9... Well known Judge Andreas Kendrick of the D.C. Superior Court is believed to be having an affair with Attorney Kennedy Glory of Weitzman, Shapiro, & Langford. Ms. Glory made partner at the firm approximately two years ago. We wonder if her relationship with the good judge had anything to do with her quick rise here in the D.C. legal world. Ms. Glory is the only African American female partner in the firm, and only the third female to ever make partner in the firm. We've reached out to the Court and Weitzman, Shapiro & Langford, but have yet to receive a comment.

My hands were shaking... hell, I was shaking. I was on the verge of tears. A quick three-minute story was getting ready to ruin my entire career, a career I worked so hard for.

I can't believe this is happening. The tears began to fall from my eyes, and it felt hard to breathe.

"Baby, what's wrong?"

I didn't even hear Andreas walk into the bedroom. Any other morning, I would have been drooling over how fine he looked bare chested and glistening with sweat. Today, however, I could barely make out his frame through the tears that continued to flow from my lids and stream down my face.

The news clip was over, but I grabbed my tablet off of the bed and googled the story. I handed him the tablet, and as he watched, more tears pooled behind my lids listening to the story for a second time. I felt like my world was being shattered into a million pieces.

Not one word from either report mentions anything negative about Andreas, but they all painted me to be some gold-digging whore, who needed connections to make it up the ladder in a world ruled by men. Every report mysteriously left off how I graduated at the top of my class from Stanford University, barred in seven fucking states, and have been with my firm since moving back to the DMV. All of those accolades didn't matter one fucking iota.

Once Andreas finished with the clips, we sat in silence for a few moments. He was probably equally as shocked… or not shocked at all.

I turned to him and asked, "Did you fucking do this, Andreas? This is what you wanted, right… to be out in the open."

A look of shock, hurt, and anger all crossed his face in what felt like a split second.

Okay… maybe he didn't do this. Shit.

Before I could even backtrack, Andreas hopped up off the bed. I could feel the rage emanating off of him.

"I know you're not fucking serious right now, Kennedy. I know you didn't just say that out of your got-damn mouth. I would never do no shit like that! Why the fuck would I hurt you like that? THE ONLY REASON I WANTED OUR SHIT OUT IN THE OPEN WAS SO THAT I CAN KISS MY FUCKING WIFE OUT IN PUBLIC, BRING HER LUNCH, TELL HER I LOVED HER!!! YOU'VE LOST YOUR FUCKING MIND ACCUSING ME OF SOME SHIT LIKE THAT!"

I have never seen Andreas this angry. Ever! We've been together for five years and married for two… not once has he even raised his voice at me. However, I couldn't fault him. Accusing him of leaking our relationship to the press was low. I also should've known it wasn't him, because if he did tell anybody anything, he would have fully claimed me as his wife. From the reports, it didn't look like they had the full story. They seemed to have no idea we were married. Someone would have had to dig really deep to obtain a copy of our marriage license filed in the State of California.

"Andreas, baby… I'm so sorry. I truly am. I know you didn't do this. I was having a meltdown and that accusation should have never left my mouth."

I hung my head low and more tears escaped. I could feel Andreas. I know he wanted to come and console me, but he was hurting too. He walked into the bathroom and I jumped when I heard the door slam.

God, life has been pretty easy for us for the past five years. Please help us get through this. I love my husband with all of my heart and don't want to lose him.

11 - Andreas

I needed to cool the hell down. I know Kennedy didn't mean that shit she said. I know she was having a meltdown. But to accuse me of going against her, my wife, my rib… my fucking world… that shit hurt.

I was going to fix this though, starting with the muthafucka that had the balls to leak this story. I just needed a cool shower to calm my nerves and fix my energy. I knew Kennedy was going to need me to be strong for her, for whatever came next.

After a long shower, I walked back into the bedroom and Kennedy was curled up in a ball still crying. Both of our phones were buzzing off of the hook. Ignoring the phones, I climbed in bed behind Kennedy and pulled her to me.

"Dre, I am so sorry for accusing you of this. Baby, I am so damn sorry," she sobbed harder, and I turned her to face me and kissed her on the forehead.

"I know, baby. I know. I'm going to fix this, you hear me?"

"No matter what we do, this will ruin me and my career."

"Shh." I attempted to ease her worries so that she would quiet her sobs. "No, it won't. I won't let it. I got you. We're going to come out of this on top."

We laid like that for as long as we could, before the buzzing of both our phones frustrated us both.

"Come on, baby. Let's start doing some damage control."

We got out of bed and put robes on. Whatever was going to be done today, would be done from the comfort of our home. I was not allowing Kennedy out of this damn house until I had a plan of action.

My first calls were to Jameela and my secretary, Renee, both of whom were aware of my and Kennedy's marriage. I called them to secure a plan of action, because I knew neither one of them were the ones to leak information to the press.

We tentatively scheduled a press conference to take place in two days. But I needed to reach out to each judge of the Advisory Committee on Judicial Conduct, and the counsel for the committee. Once those issues were cleared, I emailed Jameela and Renee to move forward with finalizing the plans for the press conference and to contact the committee counsel so that a statement can be drafted. Of course, I would alter the statement, but I needed to tend to Kennedy. I didn't want to be held up in my office drafting shit for hours and leave her to her thoughts. Kennedy had a tendency to jump off the deep end when things didn't go exactly as she planned them.

Like blaming my ass for this shit.

Yea, nah. I couldn't leave my wife alone right now.

Before going back upstairs to her, I did make a call to Joel Weitzman. We were close associates and played golf together often. I knew Kennedy hadn't made any calls yet… she could barely stop crying.

Calling him on his cell phone, opposed to at the office, Joel picked up on the first ring.

"Kendrick, you've mentioned to me over golf several times that you were a married man when I tried to point out a piece of ass. Please tell me you are not having an affair with one of my best attorneys."

I couldn't help but chuckle. Joel could be so extra. I also liked the fact that he mentioned Kennedy as being one of his best attorneys, instead of trash talking her.

"Joel, you know me better than that…"

"So, the reports aren't true? You aren't having an affair with Kennedy Glory?"

"Can't have an affair with what is already mine and has been mine for the past five years."

"HOLY FUCK!" Joel yelled. "You and Kennedy Glory are married? How the hell did this small ass city miss that?!"

"Doesn't matter at the moment. I just wanted to give you a call because Kennedy is taking this *breaking news* really bad. We're having a press conference on Friday. She'll need some time off while we get this situated."

"Kendrick, whatever she needs, man. She is literally the best damn attorney in my office. Please let me know if you two need anything. I stand behind you two and y'all have my full support."

"I appreciate that, Joel. For now, all I need is for you to keep this info wrapped up tight. Whoever did this meant to hurt Kennedy, and like everyone else, had no clue that we were married. I can tell just by the twist on the story that this was a personal attack on her. I'm going to find that muthafucka and break his got-damn face."

"Now, Judge Kendrick... don't say that to me, man. I don't want to have to testify to any of this shit in court. And we have people who can do that for you. No need to get your hands dirty."

I shook my head. Joel was a really cool guy. And even though he came from money, he tried his best to surround himself with a diverse group of people who kept him grounded.

"I'll keep that in mind, Joel. Because you know how the media is, even after our press conference, we may need you to provide a statement as well. The reporters are going to continue to run with the story that Kennedy used her connections to get her to the place she's at in her career; which we know is absolutely not true."

He agreed and assured me again, that he's ready to help

in any way possible.

"Thanks, Joel. Let me go check on Kennedy. I've been doing damage control for a while, and I don't want to leave her alone for too long."

"Sure, no problem. Tell Kennedy we have her back and fully support her through this and that her job is in no way in jeopardy."

"Thanks again, man. I'll keep you posted."

We ended the call, and I went to the kitchen to make some tea and took it to Kennedy. When I walked into the room, she was sitting on the bed staring into space.

"Kenni, baby, I made you some tea." She just stared at me.

"What are we going to do Dre? This can ruin both of our careers. I should've listened to you from jump. We should've made our situation public; people would've talked, but it wouldn't be this bad."

"Fuck them. Our shit is none of their business. And I've already made calls and set a press conference for Friday. We're going to set the record straight. I'm also going to find the person responsible for leaking this story. I promise you that everything will be okay. I even spoke with Joel."

"Shit! Work!" Kennedy was ready to jump out of bed, but I held her back.

"It's okay. Everything is fine. Joel and the firm will stand behind you, and he said take as much time as you need. He's not willing to lose you."

Kennedy's body sagged at my words. I know she was relieved to not have to worry about her job.

"Listen, Kenni. I know this shit is tough and it hurts, but I'm going to need you to be on top of your game when Friday comes. Cry that shit out today and tomorrow - I'll hold you tight while you do - but Friday morning, I need that beautiful, strong, and fierce attorney gracing that podium with me."

I grabbed her chin and turned her to face me.

"Whatever the outcome, you and I are going to be good. I don't give a fuck if we gotta leave and start over somewhere else… we got enough money to say fuck everybody in the DMV."

I got Kenni to laugh at my last comment. Even though it was short lived, it was enough to let me know that she would be alright.

12 - *Kennedy*

I have been crying all damn day. I felt like my world was being turned upside down. Andreas has been my rock through it all. He didn't leave my side, apart from the time he took to get the press conference scheduled.

"You want to go downstairs and try to put something in your stomach?" Dre asked. I didn't really have an appetite, and I just wanted to stay in bed.

"Not really. I just want to stay in bed."

"Okay. I'm going to make something quick to eat and at least bring you some crackers and ginger ale. You need to put something in your stomach."

I laughed at him and his damn ginger ale. He always perpetuated the Black stereotype that ginger ale fixed everything.

"Okay, baby."

"There's that smile I like to see."

Andreas leaned down and kissed me on the lips. It was too quick for my liking, but I let him go get food.

My mind was still reeling, and I couldn't stop thinking about the news reports. Each report got nastier and painted me in such a terrible light. Even if Andreas and I were having an affair, there was not one single bad word mentioned with regard to him. I don't understand why women were the only ones who received backlash when secret relationships and affairs came to the light. It was as if the male involved in said situation assumed none of the responsibility. It was sickening.

I don't know why I kept doing it to myself, but every hour or so, I would google us and see what, if any, new things were posted online. The newest article had me so mad, especially seeing that the journalist was a Black woman.

She Started From The Bottom; Now She's Here: All of the juicy details of Attorney Kennedy Glory growing up poor in Southeast, D.C. and finding rich men along the way to boost her up.

I was seeing red. I wanted to find Miss Chardonnay Johnson and whoop her ass.

Ghetto name having bitch! That bitch just mad she didn't have the same fate as me, and she needs to hate on other successful Black women to build up her own self-worth, I thought.

Even though I was enraged. I was still hurt and swimming in a sea of pain, and the tears wouldn't stop. Lost in the river of tears that wouldn't cease, I again didn't hear Andreas come back into the bedroom until he slipped in the bed behind me.

He took the tablet out of my hands to see what I was looking at.

"Okay, no more googling yourself. Fuck everyone and their opinion."

I sniffled and nodded.

Andreas turned me on my back and hovered over me and just stared into my eyes.

"I fucking love you, Kennedy. Everything is going to be okay," he finally spoke.

Andreas spoke those words to me, for probably the thousandth time today. I couldn't believe that all of this happened only a short twelve hours ago. He leaned down and kissed me reverently, passionately. I was dazed.

"Do you hear me, Kenni? I love you so damn much, and whatever happens doesn't mean a thing when it comes to our marriage. We're going to continue to be the same fun loving, horny ass couple we've always been."

To prove his point, Andreas snaked his hand up my waist, to my breast, and tweaked my nipple between his fingers. He continued his slow sensual kiss, and I became dizzy with need. I needed him to make me feel good, even if it were for a short time.

After removing our clothes, Andreas slid into my honeypot with slow, deep strokes, worshipping my body. His hands continued to roam all over my body as he hovered over me.

With every idolatrous thrust, Andreas whispered how much he loved me, and how beautiful I was. His words and tender care of my body brought tears to my eyes, but for different reasons from my earlier tears. Right now, I felt totally euphoric, felt loved beyond measure, safe and protected from everything and anyone. Andreas treated me like a queen, his queen, who he would die protecting.

I lost control of my body under Andreas' manipulations. He owned every inch of me, and I was starting to unravel.

"That's it, baby. See me, feel me... only me... nothing else."

Andreas bought my leg up and draped it over his shoulder, plunging deep into me. It felt like he was trying to make us one outside of the marriage sense. The way his body molded to mine, I couldn't tell where he began and I ended, and I didn't want to.

"Andreassss. I love youuu," I cried out as I jumped off the cliff into an abyss of pleasure.

"Damn, Kenni," Andreas grunted out his release.

We stayed intertwined for a little while, coming down off our high. The way Andreas loved me, for the first time throughout the day, I really felt like everything would be okay.

"Now, let's go grab a shower and get you something to eat. And I'm not trying to hear that you aren't hungry."

I listened like a dutiful wife, and Andreas tried his best to keep me relaxed for the rest of the night. And I must say, he did a pretty damn good job.

~~~~~

I woke up the next morning feeling a lot better than I had the day before. Who knew it would take a vicious attack on my character and Andreas and I's relationship to get him to miss a workout and stay in bed. I woke to his arms wrapped strongly around me, and it felt so damn good.

Andreas must've felt me moving under him, and he snuggled into my neck kissing me behind my ear… my spot.

"Don't start anything you can't finish," I told him.

"Oh, I can always finish, baby."

I wiggled from under him.

"As good as that sounds, I have to go to the bathroom."

Not to mention, that my pussy needs a break. Andreas made slow sweet love to me all damn night, and it felt amazing. However, he done drained every drop he could from my honeypot, and she needed to soak.

I took a long bath and started preparing myself for what was next to come. I cried for a day, now it was time to suck that shit up and face my problems like the vicious attorney I was.

When I walked out of the bathroom, Andreas was sitting up watching T.V.
~~~~~

"I'm going to fucking kill that muthafucka."

"Huh? You're going to kill who?" I asked him. Andreas had a killer look in his eyes and I didn't know what was going on."

"Anthony fucking Crumm. I should've known all of this shit was his doing."

"What are you talking about, Dre?" I was so fucking confused.

Andreas hit rewind on the DVR and turned the volume up. I could not believe what I was hearing. Dre was going to have to get in line behind me, because I was definitely going to kill that man.

"Well, DMV... if you've been following any news reports in the last twenty-four hours, you already know all about the scandal between Judge Andreas Kendrick and Attorney Kennedy Glory. We have an exclusive interview with someone who works closely with the two of them and we have him here on the Hot Topics segment spilling all of the tea. Welcome our guest, Attorney Anthony Crumm."

"Good morning, Mr. Crumm. Welcome to the show. How are you today?"

"I'm great. Thank you for asking."

"Let's jump right to it. You have personal knowledge of Judge Kendrick and Kennedy Glory's affair?

"Yes, ma'am I do. I always thought something was off about those two. I go up against Ms. Glory in court often and I have a one hundred percent losing record when we're before Judge Kendrick. And now I know why. Any proceeding he oversees with Kennedy, I'm sure are skewed in her favor. My cases definitely are. Judge Kendrick even likes to put on a front agreeing with Ms. Glory's opponent from time to time. I guess he has to make it look like he's not showing favoritism."

"Did you always know about their affair?"

"No, I did not. But now that I do, hindsight is twenty-twenty. The way they gaze at one another in the courtroom is beyond inappropriate. There are also several courthouse stills showing Ms. Glory leaving his chambers with a bright smile on her face. Recently Judge Kendrick was supposed to be reprimanding her for her behavior in his courtroom, but the photos released tell a different story. They both need to be held accountable for their actions and stripped of their titles. And I am going to do everything in my power to bring Ms. Glory to justice."

"You only want to bring Ms. Glory to justice? Not Judge Kendrick?"

"I'll let his peers take care of him. I'm sure his fellow judges will disapprove of the new findings."

The interview went on and on about how unprofessional

we were. About how Andreas would take me into his chambers after court proceedings to have sexual relations. He wasn't wrong there, but that had nothing to do with why he was a sore ass loser. I just kicked his ass every time because I was that damn good.

"I cannot believe this shit." I shouted. I really wanted to punch something.

"You? I'm going to sue his ass for defamation then kick his fucking ass."

"I knew I should've put his racist ass on front street long ago."

"What do you mean?" Andreas asked.

"This asshole went to Stanford with me. Jameela did some research on him a while back, and found a bunch of racist shit on his old social media accounts about how it was hard enough he had to compete with fatherless niggers, and then having to compete with nigger bitches too. I went back and looked up the ranking history of the year I graduated from Stanford, and sure enough his ass ranked under me. He's had it out for me, and I'm sure all black people, probably since birth."

"Why didn't you tell me this shit? I could've been handled his ass."

"I didn't fucking know he would do this," I said and waved my hand at the T.V.

"I'm pretty sure I heard that bastard say some racist shit when I left the cigar lounge the night he *ran* into me. I let it slide because I was on my way out and I wasn't sure he said what he said. I brushed it off to me trippin'."

"What did he say?"

"First, he called you a bitch, and I put his ass in his place. And on my way out I thought I heard him call me a *fucking nigger.*"

"Oh, I'm sure that's exactly what he said. What do you want to do?"

"We're coming for that ass during our press conference tomorrow. You still have all that social media shit?"

"I sure do, and I can ask Jameela if she looked at anything else."

"Good. Don't worry about a muthafuckin' thing. He's going to wish he loved black people when I'm through with him."

And I didn't worry. We lounged around the house the rest of the day, preparing for our press conference. I felt like a new woman, on a mission to stomp in Anthony Crumm's balls.

Oh, this is going to be fun.

13 - Andreas

We walked into the press conference with our heads held high and confidence on ten. I knew we would kill this shit. I also knew that there was going to still be a few weak-minded individuals that would still try and be against Kennedy and me. I wasn't having it though. They could all go fuck themselves.

Whoever Anthony Crumm used to obtain information on Kennedy, did a terrible job. We were getting ready to drop a bomb on everyone and take back control of this situation.

Behind us, taking seats at the table set up for the conference, was the counsel for the Advisory Committee of the Judicial Court, Jonathan Townsend, and Kennedy's boss, Joel Weitzman. Joel insisted on being by our sides to show support. He was also just as invested in bringing Anthony Crumm down. Joel provided data on every case his firm had with Anthony, and it showed he lost ninety-eight percent of his trials against the firm, among a mixed group of attorneys he went up against. Jonathan also had a case analysis done of all my trials with Kennedy. Because the court transcripts were public record, we were able to pull the jury selections, openings, closing, exhibits and everything else we needed to show that Kennedy wasn't receiving any special treatment. Jonathan had spreadsheets created, along with court transcripts, and had seventy-five copies bound to give to everyone in attendance.

Kennedy and I had, but didn't wear our wedding rings, her suggestion, not mine. However, before we left the house, I made sure to slip her three-carat pear shaped diamond ring and three-sixty diamond wedding band on her left ring finger. I also placed my simple platinum band on my finger. I didn't like how things came about, but the world was about to know Kennedy was mine.

When we sat down, cameras were flashing everywhere, and the room was buzzing. I made sure to hold my left hand up to quiet everyone down.

"Thank you all for being here on this Friday morning. I'm sure you all have better things to do," I chuckled as a round of *no's* chorused through the room. "Let's jump right into it, why don't we. There were some pretty nasty things said about Kennedy and I over the past two days. Reports on what people think they know about our situation, so please allow Kennedy and I to set the record straight."

"Judge Kendrick. I see a wedding band on your finger. Did you and Ms. Glory have a shotgun wedding after the reports?"

I laughed and rubbed my goatee.

"Absolutely not. In fact, Mrs. Glory-Kendrick and I have been married for over two years now."

A round of gasps was all that could be heard in the room.

I turned to Kennedy and brushed a stray strand of hair from her face and smiled at her. Her hand nervously traced the same pattern as mine, making sure her hair was good. The cameras went wild as they got a good view of her wedding ring.

"If the two of you have been married for years now, why keep it a secret?"

"Because as you've seen over the past few days, the world can be cruel to women, especially Black women. My beautiful wife wanted to build her success on her name alone. Which I might add, she's done exceptionally well. All of your recent reports failed to mention that my amazing wife graduated at the top of her class from Stanford University Law School, is barred in seven states and has been one of the top earning attorneys, and a well deserving partner at Weitzman, Shapiro & Langford. Every single report failed to mention those accolades… accolades Kennedy has earned on her own, without the help of any man and definitely without the help of my last name."

Every reporter in the room suddenly got quiet at that statement, but not for long.

"Judge Kendrick. I just did a search of court records in the DMV and there's no recordings of your and Ms. Glory's marriage."

The reporter had a smirk on his face, as if we were lying. I smirked back at the bastard.

"Well if everyone here did a better job of researching a story before going public, records of our marriage certificate would've been found in a public docket search in the State of California." I didn't even waste my time elaborating any further.

Since there was no drama and scandal to focus on with that line of questioning, the reporters moved on.

"Kennedy, what do you think of Attorney Anthony Crumm's interview regarding you and Judge Kendrick's relationship."

Before Kennedy could even speak, I stepped in.

"First, as you have addressed me with the respect my title deserves, as Judge Kendrick, you will address my wife with the same respect. Thus, moving forward in this press conference, you will refer to her as Attorney Glory, Mrs. Glory, or Mrs. Glory-Kendrick. However, no one is to address her by Kennedy as if you know her personally."

I turned to Kennedy and winked at her, and she smiled back at me, causing more camera flashes.

"Mrs. Glory, I apologize... I meant no disrespect. How do you feel with regards to Anthony Crumm's exclusive interview?"

"Mr. Crumm has had it out for me for quite some time

now. I only became recently aware that his hatred towards me went back further than our time here in the DMV. Mr. Crumm and I went to Stanford University together, where I graduated ahead of him. Honestly, I don't even remember Mr. Crumm. However, after one of his many disrespectful rants directed my way, my amazing and dutiful assistant did some research into Mr. Crumm. What we found is rather horrifying. It became painfully clear that Mr. Crumm has it out for Black people, and even more so for Black women. I took the liberty of printing copies of old racist posts from Mr. Crumm's social media account."

I waved at my secretary and Jameela to pass out the pages of offensive social media posts from Anthony. Once everyone had a copy, Kennedy continued.

"As you can see, the posts are rather vulgar. As such, both my husband and I plan on filing defamation lawsuits against Mr. Crumm."

As every reporter took a moment to read over the document they were just handed, you could see the anger emerge on the face of every Black person in the room.

"Also, before anyone question my fairness, I'll wrap up this press conference by saying that Jonathan Townsend, the attorney for the Advisory Committee on Judicial Conduct, has prepared a detailed report of the cases I presided over with my wife. There is an abundance of information that one hundred percent proves each and every one of Mr. Crumm's allegations are completely false. This will be another reason we file a defamation lawsuit. Mr. Crumm has made himself very clear on heading a fictitious witch hunt involving my wife and I. To that end, we will ensure Mr. Crumm does not walk away from this unscathed. We have already filed a grievance with the District of Columbia Bar and the Board on Professional Responsibility, along with the lawsuit we will be filing. Mr. Crumm needs to be held accountable for his words and actions. Please feel free to read through the large reports we've prepared for you and report on factual information moving forward.

Again, thank you for showing up here today and allowing my wife and I to set the record straight. You all enjoy the rest of your day and weekend."

I held my hand out for Kennedy and we made our way out the space. Leaving all that shit behind us. I wasn't worried about anything else regarding the matter. I just publicly buried the muthafucka who thought he was going to hurt my wife, and next I was going to bankrupt his ass just for the hell of it and donate any monetary reward to the Black community.

I was going to love taking every racist ass penny he had and invest it into the community and group of people he hated so much.

I've been behind the bench so long that I forgot the rush

that came with kicking someone's ass in the court of law. Victory ain't never felt so good.

Now, I was going to leave here and take my wife to the fanciest fucking restaurant in town and put our love on full display for everyone to witness. Then I was going to take her ass home and make passionate love to her all damn weekend.

THE END

www.ingramcontent.com/pod-product-compliance
Ingram Content Group UK Ltd.
Pitfield, Milton Keynes, MK11 3LW, UK
UKHW041644190726
13854UKWH00006B/2680

9 781716 017094